May I Hel...

MANNERS ALWAYS MATTER

Illustrated by Lance Raichert
Written by Jason Blundy

Mouse, Kitty, Bunny, Puppy, and Bear walked to school together every day.

They usually spent their time joking and laughing all the way, but one day they noticed an old house that was falling apart.

"It's a shame," said Kitty. "I wonder why no one does anything to fix that house."

That day at school Mrs. Hen taught the class about community and how it is important to help others. Mrs. Hen's lesson gave Bunny an idea.

"Excuse me, Mrs. Hen," said Bunny, "but we know of someone who could really use our help. There's a house down the street that is in real need of repairs. Maybe we could help."

Mrs. Hen was delighted to hear that her students understood her lesson and that they wanted to help. She thought for a moment.

"Since you are all such good students, and because you are so willing to help, I think today would be a good day for a field trip," she said.

With that the students jumped to their feet in excitement.

The students raced to the house down the street. Mrs. Panda greeted them cheerily.

"Mrs. Panda," said Mouse, "we wonder if you might like for us to help fix up your house?"

"Why . . . yes," said Mrs. Panda.

Immediately, the students began happily working around the house, fixing broken doors and tidying the yard.

Mouse felt bad because she was too small to help with the big chores.

"Excuse me, Mrs. Panda, but would you mind if I read you a story?" asked Mouse.

"I think that would be delightful, little one," said Mrs. Panda with a smile.

So Mouse read Mrs. Panda her favorite story while the others finished working on the house.

After all of the work was finished, Mrs. Panda looked around in amazement.

"I must say you young ones are such a pleasure," she said.

"The pleasure was all ours," said Puppy.

"Well, thank you all very much," said Mrs. Panda. "Please wait here for just a minute."

Mrs. Panda went inside the house for a moment and then returned with treats.

"Please take these for your walk back to school," said Mrs. Panda. "I would hate for such generosity to go unrewarded."

"Thank you. We will enjoy them," said Mouse. "But helping you was reward enough for us."

May I Help?

No one likes to have to ask for help. That's why it is always nice to offer a helping hand. As Mouse and her friends learned, it not only makes the person being helped feel good, but makes the helpers feel great, too!